THE ARABIAN NIGHTS

CHILDREN'S COLLECTION

Dados Internacionais de Catalogação na Publicação (CIP) de acordo com ISBD

J76g   Jones, Kellie
         Gulnare of the sea / adaptado por Kellie Jones. – Jandira : W. Books, 2025.
         168 p. ; 12,8cm x 19,8cm. – (The Arabian nights)

         ISBN: 978-65-5294-181-7

         1. Literatura infantojuvenil. 2. Contos. 3. Contos de Fadas. 4. Literatura Infantil.
         5. Clássicos. 6. Mágica. 7. Histórias. I. Título. II. Série.

2025-596   CDD 028.5
                                                                CDU 82-93

Elaborado por Vagner Rodolfo da Silva - CRB-8/9410
Índice para catálogo sistemático:
1. Literatura infantojuvenil 028.5
2. Literatura infantojuvenil 82-93

The Arabian Nights 10 Book Collection
Text © Sweet Cherry Publishing Limited, 2023
Inside illustrations © Sweet Cherry Publishing Limited, 2023
Cover illustrations © Sweet Cherry Publishing Limited, 2023

Text based on translations of the original folk tale,
adapted by Kellie Jones
Illustrations by Arianna Bellucci

© 2025 edition:
Ciranda Cultural Editora e Distribuidora Ltda.

1st edition in 2025
www.cirandacultural.com.br
No part of this publication may be reproduced, stored in a retrieval
system, or transmitted in any form or by any means, electronic,
mechanical, photocopying, recording, or otherwise, without written
permission of the publisher.
This book is a work of fiction. Names, characters, places, and incidents
are either the product of the author's imagination or are used fictitiously,
and any resemblance to actual persons, living or dead, business
establishments, events, or locales is entirely coincidental.

Long ago, in the ancient lands of Arabia, there lived a brave woman called Scheherazade. When the country's sultan went mad, Scheherazade used her cleverness and creativity to save many lives – including her own. She did this over a thousand and one nights, by telling the sultan stories of adventure, danger and enchantment.

These are just some of them …

King Hamid

A lonely man who loves the sea

Princess Gulnare

Rose of the Sea

Prince Beder

Gulnare's son

King Saleh

Gulnare's brother

Queen Farasche

Gulnare and Saleh's mother

King Samandal

A neighbouring sea king

Princess Giauhara

Samandal's daughter

Queen Labe

A sorceress

Abdallah

A kind fruit seller

Chapter 1

The Story of the King and the Silent Woman

There was once a king of Persia who, after winning many battles, was enjoying some well-deserved peace. The people he ruled over were happy. The land he ruled over was rich. And the palace he lived in was by the sea, which he loved.

The king's only source of sadness was that he had no family to live

> **Persia**
> *An ancient empire in southwestern Asia, now called Iran.*

in the palace with him, nor a son to rule his kingdom after he was gone. Until now, he had always been too busy to think of such things. He regretted that he might have left it too late.

One night there was a terrible storm. The king watched from the palace as the sea battered the shore, and in the morning a woman was found washed up on the beach. Since no one knew who she was and she would not tell them, the woman was brought to the palace.

The king was startled by her

appearance. Her face was uncovered and her hair fell in waves all the way to the ground, so black that it had a bluish sheen to it. Her eyes, meanwhile, were an ever-changing shade of greenish blue-grey. She was tall – almost as tall as him – and broad-shouldered. She looked strong, despite the fact that she was wobbling on her feet. She did not bow to him so much as fall down in front of his throne.

'Bring a chair,' the king commanded a servant, and one was brought. As the woman sat in it, she seemed more interested in the chair than the king. She bounced lightly on the cushion and ran her fingers along the decorative wooden armrests.

'What is your name?' the king asked her. She did not answer. 'My name is King Hamid.'

The woman's eyes roved around the throne room, which was famous for having so many windows that there were almost no walls left.

'You are in Bushehr,' Hamid continued, 'in Persia. Where are you from?' Her clothes gave him no clue to the answer. Her long dress was made of a loose, pale, shimmering material that changed colour almost as often as her eyes did. It was like the inside of a shell, and it moved around her like water. She wore no shoes and had on a strange necklace made from sea glass. The proud tilt of her head alone suggested that she came from a wealthy family – maybe even royalty.

'Can you speak?' Hamid asked. He tried asking the same question in a few other languages.

The woman gasped as her eyes fell on the sea view outside the windows. Then she leapt up and ran towards it – or tried to. Her feet tangled together halfway and she fell to the floor again. Hamid helped her up. Her hands were soft; not like the hands of a servant or other working woman.

'Prepare a room for her,' he commanded the same servant as before. Then, seeing how the woman continued to gaze at the sea, he added, 'Choose one with the best view.'

The king had decided to keep the woman at the palace until she recovered. Whether she was rich or not, he owed her his protection. Plus he was very curious about her.

When the room was ready, Hamid led her there himself. One wall had a window so large that it seemed to frame the entire ocean beyond it. Whisper-thin net curtains blew into the room, which was tiled all over in shades of green, turquoise and blue. Only the floor was a pale brown colour, like polished sand.

'You can stay here,' Hamid said kindly. 'My servants will bring you a change of clothes and some food.

Unless you would like to dine with me?'

The woman did not reply.

'Very well, if you change your mind, come anyway. I am always grateful to have company.'

But the woman did not go to the king. She spent the next three days alone, dressed in the finest clothes, sitting in the same place, which was a chair on the balcony.

Eventually Hamid went to see her himself. When he found her on the balcony, she did not stand to greet him. In fact she barely glanced at him before returning her attention to the sea. Her hair had been brushed and piled on top of her head. Around it was a circlet of pearls to match a pearl necklace. She looked like royalty, but she did not seem to know how to behave towards a king. Fortunately, Hamid did not mind. He was already surrounded by people who lived to please him. He did not need another.

He decided to be more relaxed too. Rather than waiting for a servant to do it for him, he pulled a second chair onto the balcony beside his guest. They sat together in silence for a while before he felt the need to fill it.

'Clearly you love the sea as much as I do,' he said. 'Most of my battles were fought on land, but if you look over there when the tide is low there are several shipwrecks.

That is where my enemies tried to invade many years ago.'

The woman looked where he pointed but did not reply.

On future visits, the king spoke about the sea, the palace, the land, the people and finally about himself. He told the woman everything about himself that he wanted to know about her: his likes and dislikes, hopes and fears; his dreams. After many weeks he found that he did not have much else to say, so the two sat in comfortable silence – at least

invade
When one country or area attacks another country or area in order to rule over it.

he thought it was a comfortable silence. But he began to worry that the woman might feel differently.

'Has she spoken at all?' he asked the servants. 'Is it just me she ignores?'

'No, Your Majesty,' they reassured him. 'She has never said a word to anyone. We bring her food and fix her hair, but she dresses herself in her own style as she pleases. She never asks for or complains about anything.'

On his next visit, Hamid asked the woman herself: 'Do my visits bother you? If they do, you must tell me or show me and I will not come again.'

When as usual she did not answer, the king stood to leave. But the woman caught his hand and stopped him. She looked up at him, and to his surprise, she smiled. To his utter delight, she spoke.

'No,' she said.

'No?' the king repeated. 'As in, *no* my visits do not bother you?'

'No.'

She would not say more, but she seemed pleased when he returned to his chair beside her. So the visits continued. Now that

Hamid knew she understood what he was saying, he began bringing books from his library to give him something to talk about. The woman began to look at him more. She now nodded to him when he came and went.

One day he brought a map and pointed to the land where they were. 'This is us,' he said. 'Show me, where are you from?'

The woman pointed at the part of the map that showed the sea. The king studied the blue area.

'Should there be an island here?' he asked. 'New islands are being discovered every day. Perhaps yours is not on the map yet.'

'No,' she said.

'No, you are not from an island?'

'Yes.'

The woman began to answer Hamid in yeses and nos. 'Are you cold?' 'No.' 'Are you hungry?' 'Yes.' 'Are you happy?' 'Yes.' This

last answer pleased the king very much, for he was happy too.

When the woman had been with him for many months, he asked, 'Will you marry me?'

'Why?'

The king was surprised to hear her say a new word. 'Because I love you.'

'You do not know me.'

This was more than the woman had ever said before. 'So you can speak!' Hamid cried. 'Why have you not spoken properly before?'

The woman answered slowly and carefully, as if she was

choosing the right words in the right order. 'At first … I was sad about losing my home. Then I waited to see what kind of man you were. Then I had to learn your language.'

'You speak it beautifully!' the king seized her hands and kissed them. 'I have longed for you to talk to me. Please, tell me everything. What is your name? Where are you from? Who are your family? How did you lose your home?'

'I can answer all those questions in one short story …'

Chapter 2

The Story of Gulnare of the Sea

My name is Gulnare, Rose of the Sea. My father was a king of the ocean and my mother a queen. When my father died, my brother Saleh took over his responsibilities.

Saleh was a good king and our underwater kingdom was peaceful. I wish you could have seen it. Our palace

is even more beautiful than this one, with towers that spiral like a narwhal's tusk and rooms modelled after all sorts of sea shells. There is coral bigger than your oldest trees and reefs more colourful than your brightest flowers. Our music is whale song and our sport is surfing the currents. But it hurts to speak of all that now.

One day, a neighbouring prince grew jealous of our happiness. He invaded with a mighty army and took our capital city for himself.

narwhal
A type of whale with a long tusk growing through its upper lip.

current
The direction and flow of water.

Saleh, my mother and I barely escaped with our lives and some of our people.

My brother tried to take the city back by force many times. With each failure more men and women died. Saleh grew so angry that I hardly recognised him.

'Let me try,' I begged. 'Let me help you. I will talk to the prince and try to reason with him.'

'I do not want you anywhere near him!' he said. 'In return for peace he will ask for your hand in marriage. But our father did not just leave me the kingdom to

protect, he left me you as well.
I must keep you safe.'

'But I want to fight!'

'*No.*'

It was bad enough that he would not let me help; the worst thing was that he would not even let me stay. Saleh decided that I would be safer on land than in the sea. He ordered soldiers to take me to the surface and leave me there, which they did. I swam home, of course. I swam home many times. On the final time, my brother dragged me back to the surface himself. Over the roar of a storm, he gave me an order: 'Do not come back until the fighting is over. As your king, I forbid it.'

The storm took me and brought me to a strange shore – *your* shore. When I was brought to the palace, I thought I had been taken prisoner. I could not walk well enough to escape, and even if I did escape, where would I go? Back to the sea? My brother forbids it. And then I realised that I was not a prisoner but a guest ... and ... perhaps something more ...

You already know the rest of the story ...

King Hamid was not surprised to
learn that the woman – *Gulnare* –
was a princess. But a princess of
the sea? *That* was unexpected.
He kissed her hands again.

'Something more than a guest?'
he repeated. 'Far more indeed!
You are more than anything I
ever dreamt of, and yet I feel as
if I have always loved you. It is as
if each time I looked at the sea,
I was looking at you. It is a miracle
that we have finally met, and I am
sorry that it took such misfortune

to bring you to me. Now that you are here, will you stay? As my wife?'

'What if I say no?'

'Then you can still stay here, or I will return you to the sea myself and continue to love you every time I look at it. Then when I die, I will be buried there and we will be together again.'

Gulnare shook her head. 'I do not like to think of you dying.'

'I do not like to think of you leaving,' the king replied.

'But you would let me? If I wished to?'

'I do not believe I could stop you! And I would not try. Now and forever, you are free to come and go as you please.'

To show he was telling the truth, the king suggested that Gulnare leave the palace and visit the sea shore where she had been found. Gulnare agreed and all the time that she was gone, Hamid worried that she would not return. But she did. The next day was the same. Just like the tide, Gulnare came and went, came and went.

One day she invited Hamid to go with her, and the pair walked along the sand together. Or at least Hamid walked along the sand. Gulnare could not resist having her feet in the water as it lapped onto the beach. The king studied her bare toes.

'When you came here,' he said, 'you could not walk. How did you move around when you were underwater?'

'I swam, of course!'

'Like I do? With arms and legs?'

'Why? Did you think I might have a fish tail and fins?'

Hamid laughed. 'I would not care if you did!'

'What about our children? Would you care if they had a fish tail instead of legs?'

Hamid stopped walking. The way hope surged in his chest, he almost stopped *breathing*.

'*Our* children?' he said.

Gulnare stopped walking too.

'I miss my home very much,' she said, with her eyes on the sea. 'But if I return there now, I will be leaving my heart here on land.' She looked at Hamid. 'With you.'

'You love me?' the king gasped.

'Yes.'

'Then ... will you marry me?'

'Yes.'

He wiped tears from his eyes. 'Are you sure you have not just forgotten all the other words I taught you?'

'No.'

The pair laughed and kissed and then grew more serious.

'Will you invite your brother to the wedding?' Hamid asked her.

Gulnare sighed. 'I do not even know if he is alive. If he is, I do not know if I can forgive him for making me leave. I am happy that it brought me to you, but I am still so angry that he stole my choice.

If you had done the same, I would have left.'

'Is there no one else you want there?' he asked her. 'If there was a neighbouring prince then there

must be neighbouring lands? Other kingdoms?'

'Yes, there are many nations underwater. We have our own cities and towns, farmlands and fields, customs and culture. But I do not need anyone at our wedding besides you.'

Hamid's answer was to kiss her again.

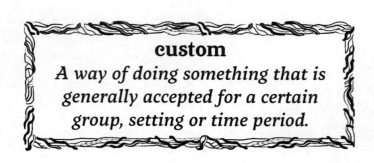

custom
A way of doing something that is generally accepted for a certain group, setting or time period.

Chapter 3

The Story of Gulnare of the Sea Continued

They were married soon after in a small ceremony by the sea. Queen Gulnare wore pearls, even though she had now told her husband that they were not considered valuable underwater, unlike sea glass.

After their wedding, Gulnare continued her walks on the beach, often with her husband beside her. They collected sea shells together.

Gulnare began using them and a piece of driftwood to make a crown.

'Who is that for?' King Hamid asked one day, coming to stand behind her as she worked. He assumed that the crown must be for him, although he already had one.

His wife shocked him by saying, 'It is for our child.'

'*You are pregnant?*'

'Yes.'

The king hugged her tightly. 'I never knew I could be this happy!' he cried.

'Nor did I,' Gulnare smiled. 'I am much too happy to stay angry at my brother. And I need to know if our child still has an uncle. I must see him. And my mother.'

'Of course, but …' Hamid hesitated. 'Forgive me, I swore I would never stop you and I will not, but if your brother's kingdom is still at war, I fear for your safety if you go to them – especially now.'

'I understand, my love. But do not worry, I have a way to contact them without going anywhere.'

The queen ordered one of the

servants to bring her a brazier. When she was alone with the king, she took a piece of sweet-smelling wood and burnt it in the brazier. Then she spoke words into the smoke that her husband could not understand – words from her underwater home.

Sometime later, the sea outside the windows began to froth and foam. In a chariot made from a giant shell and pulled by dolphins, a tall, handsome man appeared.

'It is my brother!' Gulnare gasped. 'Let us go and meet him on the beach.'

Watching from the sand, Hamid could see the resemblance as the sea king drew closer. King Saleh had the same fine features and pale skin as his sister, with blue-black hair bound under a crown of white coral. He was

brazier
A metal container for burning wood or coals. It is used for cooking or heating.

not alone. Behind him came an older woman, and a small army of men and women who looked as strong and as fierce as he did. All of the sea people wore silver-blue armour that seemed to flow around their bodies like liquid metal. Their helmets were shells, and instead of swords or spears, they carried tridents.

Saleh strode straight out of the water, showing none of the difficulty walking that his sister had shown.

Gulnare was surprised.

trident
A weapon like a spear with three sharp points at the end.

'Brother, how did you learn to walk on land?'

'By searching everywhere for you!' he said. 'I must have walked every shore but this one since the day I won back our kingdom.'

'You mean the war is over?'

'Yes, for months now. I thought you would come home or contact me sooner.'

'You were the one who sent me away,' Gulnare pointed out.

'For your own good!' Saleh replied. 'You were meant to come home once the fighting was done.'

'Well, I have a new home now.'

'So I see.' Saleh looked up at the palace. Then his attention fell on Hamid who was waiting nearby, unable to understand a word that was being said. All Hamid knew was that the sea king did not look happy.

'Who is this human?' Saleh asked his sister.

'He is the king of this land and my husband.'

'You married without asking me?' Saleh gaped at Gulnare.

'You sent me away without asking *me*,' she replied.

'I told you it was for your own good!'

'So is this! I have never been happier!'

The siblings glared at each other. Saleh looked away first and folded his arms. 'Very well.

If you are so happy, why have you contacted me?'

Gulnare softened her voice. 'You are going to be an uncle. If I have a son, I will name him after our father. If I have a daughter, I will name her after our mother. Either way, they will love you as I do.'

Saleh uncrossed his arms and looked instantly less angry. 'Then … you forgive me for sending you away?'

'Do you understand that it was wrong?'

'Yes, but truly, Gulnare, I thought it was for the best. I am sorry.'

'Then I forgive you.'

Hamid was surprised when they suddenly hugged each other. After such an intense talk, Hamid thought the sea king might have been trying to convince his sister to return with him. If so, Gulnare might have just agreed.

'Come here, my love,' she said, inviting Hamid closer in words he understood. 'This is my brother King Saleh. Saleh, this is my husband, King Hamid. And this this is my mother, former Queen Farasche.'

At last, the older woman came forward and hugged her daughter. Hamid used the few words his wife had taught him of her language. Saleh used the few words of Persian he had learnt in neighbouring lands while looking for his sister. Between that and Gulnare's translation, they managed to hold a conversation.

A picnic was set up on the beach, where the sea people sat cross-legged on the sand. Hamid joined them as more and more food was brought from the palace. There were vegetables with fruit, chicken with saffron and lamb with lemon. There were stews that were green from the number of herbs and spiced meat that made the visitors' tongues tingle. From barley to beans and pomegranates to pistachios, through to artichokes, carrots, aubergines, spinach and squash – the food overflowed.

The only thing missing was seafood, which Hamid told the servants not to bring.

'I do not think any seafood I could serve would be as good as what your people are used to,' he explained to his wife in a whisper. Gulnare laughingly agreed. Now that her two worlds had been brought together, her happiness was almost complete. A few months later it *was* complete.

The queen gave birth to a baby boy, whom she named Beder after her father. Saleh came on land to meet his new nephew. Their mother,

Farasche, was already there, having stayed with Gulnare for the final months of her pregnancy.

This time Saleh did not stay on the beach but entered the palace where his sister lay in bed recovering.

'He is perfect!' said their mother, rocking little Prince Beder and gazing at him adoringly.

'He is the best of the land *and* of the sea,' Saleh agreed when it was his turn to hold the baby.

During this turn, Beder started crying. Saleh carried him several times around the royal bedroom to calm him, but Beder would not stop. Eventually Saleh carried him out onto the huge balcony, and the crying eased a little. Then Saleh carried him right up to the edge of the balcony and peered over into the sea below.

Hamid, who had been glowing with happiness and pride all this time, now watched nervously. To his wife he said, 'He is standing very close to the edge, my dear …'

'Do not worry,' Gulnare soothed him. 'Saleh would never let any harm come to our son.'

Hamid nodded, but his belief

was tested when Saleh suddenly jumped off the balcony.

'*What is he doing?*' Hamid raced to the edge of the balcony. When he looked down into the sea, all he saw was white foam and ripples. 'They are gone!' He looked back at Gulnare who was frowning.

'Mother, *I* wanted to be the one to take Beder for his first swim!'

Farasche patted her daughter's hand soothingly. To the panicked Hamid she said, 'Gulnare was right, Saleh would never let any harm come to your son. They will be back soon.'

"Soon" felt like forever to Hamid. But it was only ten minutes later that Saleh returned with a much calmer Beder in his arms. Hamid rushed to take him.

'Remember,' Saleh said when he saw the fear and relief on Hamid's face, 'your son is also my nephew: he belongs in my kingdom just as much as in yours. He is welcome to come and go as he pleases.'

'So are you,' Hamid said. 'I hope you will stay as long as you like and visit as often as you can.'

In the end, Saleh stayed on land longer than anyone expected.

When it was time for him and his mother to return to their underwater kingdom, Hamid and Gulnare went to the beach to wave them off.

When he was up to his waist in water, Saleh asked his sister one last time, 'Are you sure you want to stay here?'

Gulnare answered, 'Yes.'

Then she said goodbye to her brother, her mother and her old life, and set out on a whole new chapter with her husband and son.

Chapter 4

The Story of Prince Beder and Princess Giauhara

The next and happiest chapter of Queen Gulnare's life lasted for fifteen years. Over those years she watched her son learn and grow, visited often by his uncle, grandmother and cousins from the sea.

As a child of two worlds, Prince Beder was kind and accepting to everyone, and the people loved him.

By the time he was fifteen, he had his mother's cleverness and his father's calm; her colour-changing eyes and his brown skin.

King Hamid was growing old, and he did not want to wait until his death to make Beder king after him. With the agreement of his advisors, Prince Beder became King Beder and Queen Gulnare became the queen mother.

For the first year of his reign, Beder stayed home in the capital and learnt, with the help of his parents, how to make his people happy. In the second year, he left the capital to visit the rest of his kingdom and do the same there. At the start of the third year, he received news that his father was ill and would not recover, so he returned home.

The late Hamid died peacefully with his wife and son beside him. King Saleh, Queen Farasche and their other sea relations came to the funeral. It was custom in Persia to spend over a month mourning a lost loved one, but Beder was so sad that it seemed like he would mourn forever.

Eventually his mother went to him in his room and said, 'My dear it is time to return to your work. You must show yourself to the people. They miss you.'

'I miss father.'

'I miss him too.' Gulnare kissed his forehead. 'But he is still here: in this palace he had built, the kingdom he helped make, the people who grew up or were born

mourning
The feeling and expression of great sadness that follows a death or loss.

during his time as king. And in *you*, especially. Hamid always said that you were born a king not a prince.'

'He was always there to advise me.'

'Just as I am here now,' said Gulnare.

With Gulnare's help, Beder returned to the work of ruling his kingdom. He did so well that his reputation for fairness and generosity spread not just across the land but through the sea. Until one day his uncle, Saleh, paid him a surprise visit.

He praised Beder so highly that the young man blushed and had to leave the room. Then Saleh turned to his sister and said, 'Why have you not found a wife for him yet? He is twenty now. If you cannot think of a princess on land, I will suggest one from the sea.'

The queen mother was taken aback. She still thought of her son as a boy, but he was old enough to marry. 'You are right,' she said. 'Beder is no longer a child. I like the idea of him marrying someone from our home. Who do you suggest?'

'Do you remember Princess Giauhara? She was a baby when you left the sea.'

'The daughter of King Samandal? How could I forget such an adorable little girl! Is she not married already?'

'No.' King Saleh sighed. 'Her father still thinks that he and his family are better than everyone else. He has rejected all of the princess's suitors, and he will probably reject Beder as well.'

'Perhaps not,' the queen mother said; 'not if he meets Beder first.

suitor
Someone who wants to marry someone specific.

Even the vain King Samandal should be able to see how kind and kingly he is.'

'Then you want me to take Beder under the sea with me?'

'Yes, but do not tell him why. I do not want him to be disappointed if he cannot marry Princess Giauhara after all.'

The only thing left was to convince Beder. He took his work very seriously and rarely took time off. But he had also wanted to see his mother's underwater kingdom his whole life. His mother reassured him, 'I can take care of the people while you are gone.'

'I wish you could come with me,' he said.

'Then you will come?' asked Saleh.

'Yes.'

Beder had always been as comfortable in water as he was out of it. He could breathe just as well there as on land and swim almost as fast as he could run. Still, he struggled to keep up with his uncle, who sliced through the water like a warm blade through ghee. Saleh did

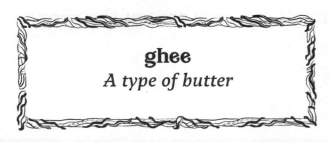

ghee
A type of butter

not want to waste any time, so
he sent word to his kingdom
by sailfish. The sailfish was the
fastest of all the sea creatures,
with a nose like a sword and top
fin like a ship's sail. It sped away
with the news that the king was
coming with his nephew.

They stopped twice to rest,
once in a cave and the second
time in a shipwreck. Then, after
swimming through a forest of
coral, they reached a white palace
guarded by sharks. It had towers
like tusks and rooms like shells,
with gardens of sea grass and

strange plants that opened and closed as they passed. At Saleh's return, thousands of multi-coloured fish swam up from the sea floor like fireworks into the sky.

Beder was reunited with his grandmother, Farasche, who was now too old to swim to the shore to see him. When Saleh told her that he wanted his nephew to marry Giauhara, she laughed.

'And how do you plan to convince the high and mighty King Samandal of that?' she

wondered. 'There is a reason no one has bothered asking for her hand in marriage these past two years. She could have been married ten times by now, but her father always says no.'

'Exactly,' said Saleh. 'If there are no sea princes good enough for her, perhaps a king of the land is what is needed. I will take a gift and tell King Samandal all about Beder and his success above the sea. Then I will invite him to dine with us and introduce them in person.'

'You will have to watch what you say. King Samandal's temper is said to sting like a jellyfish. And he *never* forgets. Just like … like a – what is that land creature with the long nose?'

'A giraffe?'

Beder reappeared at that moment. He had been exploring with his cousins. They had just introduced him to their only servant: an octopus with a tentacle serving in each part of the palace.

'This place is amazing!' he cried.

'I am glad you think so!' Saleh smiled. 'I will leave you to enjoy yourself. I must visit one of our neighbours.'

Saleh prepared
a gift of diamonds,
emeralds and rubies
that he had collected
from shipwrecks, plus glass
objects that he had brought back
from the surface over the years.
All of them were unbroken, which
was rare under the sea. He took
these to Samandal's palace with a
small company of guards.

'What brings you here?' the
older king greeted him. He sat
cross-legged on his throne, which
was a giant open clam shell on
a rock that allowed him to look

down on everyone. On his head
was a jagged crown of shark teeth.
His hair and beard were green like
seaweed.

'I have a gift for you,'
Saleh answered him.

A servant carried the gift
to Samandal. He ignored the
jewels but seemed impressed
by the glassware. He put one piece
on his head and another over his
wrist, while Saleh tried to hide his
amusement. Once, he had known
just as little about these objects
as Samandal did. Now, seeing a
bowl treated like a hat and a jug

like a bracelet made him bite his lip to keep from laughing. Despite Saleh's efforts, a small snigger escaped him when Samandal held a squat, round-bottomed bottle up to his eye by the neck and looked through it.

Samandal heard him and put the bottle down with a frown. He waved the servant away.

'Well?' he said. 'What do you expect in return for this treasure? Nothing is ever free.'

'True, Your Majesty,' Saleh said. 'I offer treasure for a treasure. I have heard much about the sweetness and beauty of your daughter, Princess Giauhara. I would like to suggest a marriage.'

Samandal could not have looked more surprised if Saleh had suggested a dance. Or more insulted.

'*You wish to marry my daughter?*'

Whereas Saleh had tried to hide his laughter, Samandal did not. He laughed loud and hard. And now it was Saleh's turn to be insulted.

'What under the sea,' Samandal choked, 'makes you think that you are worthy of marrying *my* daughter?'

'I am a king the same as you,' Saleh replied, before he could remember his mother's advice and think better of it.

Samandal jumped to his feet. 'The same as me? *The same as*

me? My kingdom is twice as big as yours!'

'And half as beautiful.'

'At least I never lost it to an invader.'

'That was years ago and I won it back again!'

'Only after running away with your mother and sister like a child!'

Samandal had come down from his throne now and the two men were nose to nose in anger. Saleh realised that his few guards and Samandal's many had their hands on their weapons in case fighting broke out. He needed to calm the situation down.

He swallowed his anger and lowered his voice. 'Worthy or not, I was not suggesting that *I* marry her.'

'Who then?'

'Perhaps you have heard that I have a nephew?'

The king laughed again. 'So rather than marry a king of the sea you want Giauhara to marry a prince of the land?'

'A *king*,' Saleh corrected him, which only made Samandal

angrier: he hated being corrected.

'A *land* king,' he said. 'I hate land people! More and more of them disturb our waters instead of staying where they belong.'

'His name is King Beder,' Saleh said. 'I am sure you have heard how loved he is by his people for his good sense and warm heart.'

'He sounds like a weakling! I do not rule by kindness but by strength.'

Saleh was even angrier at the insult to his nephew than the one to himself. 'Perhaps that is why your people do not love you the way my nephew's people love him! Then again, I suppose you do not need their love when you love yourself as much as you do.'

For a moment, neither king said anything. The words seemed to echo around the rock palace far too many times for Saleh to ever take them all back, even if he wished to – which he did not.

Samandal pointed his trident furiously at Saleh.

'Guards!' he yelled. 'Seize this fool!'

Chapter 5

The Story of King Beder and Princess Giauhara Continued

At King Samandal's command, his guards leapt towards King Saleh. With a clash of tridents, Saleh's guards fought them off, but they were outnumbered.

'Retreat!' cried Saleh.

Luckily, Saleh's mother had been worried enough about Samandal's reaction that she had sent extra

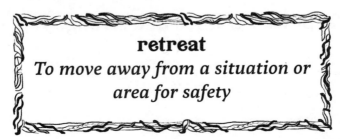

retreat
To move away from a situation or area for safety

soldiers just in case. They arrived on giant seahorses in time to find Salah and his guards being chased from the palace.

As Samandal had so rudely pointed out, Saleh had once lost his kingdom to an invader. Since that defeat, his army had been kept well-trained and strong.

Even though Samandal's kingdom was bigger, his army was not. And as Saleh had also pointed out, Samandal's people did not like him. They had no wish to die for a king they did not believe in; one who had yelled at, taken for granted and otherwise mistreated them for years. They soon stopped fighting.

Afterwards, Saleh re-entered the palace. He found Samandal alone, having been abandoned by the palace staff too.

'How dare you!' he roared. 'I will have your head for this!'

'I came here in peace,' Saleh reminded him. 'I did not want a war between our families, I wanted a wedding!'

In answer, Samandal threw his trident at him. Saleh dodged easily.

'Guards,' Saleh growled. 'Seize this fool, and find his daughter.'

But the princess, overhearing the fighting, had fled her tower for the surface and a nearby deserted island.

When news of what had happened reached Saleh's kingdom, King Beder's grandmother had no choice but to tell him.

'But I never asked to marry
Princess Giauhara!' he cried.

'It was your uncle and mother's
wish to find you the best wife,' said
Farasche, 'and Princess Giauhara
is lovely.'

'Lovely enough to go to war
over?' Beder asked.

'That was not the plan, no.'

'But that is what happened!'
Realising that he was shouting,
Beder took a deep breath. 'Forgive
me, grandmother. I am upset.
I will go and cool my head.'

When Beder was on land,
the place he went to calm down

was the sea. Now that he was already in the sea, however, he found himself seeking the land. The nearest place was an island, no longer deserted. Under the branches of a large tree, a woman was crying.

'Hello?' Beder called out in Persian, not wanting to approach and startle her. The woman was startled anyway. As she jumped up, Beder saw that she wore a large shell around her neck. Her hair, which had looked brown in the shade, was green like seaweed.

'Who are you?' he asked next.

This time he used the language of the sea people, for her hair marked her as one of them.

At the familiar words, the princess looked relieved. 'Thank goodness!' she sniffled. 'I thought you were a land person! My father tells me they are greedy and dangerous.'

'And your father is …?' But Beder suspected he already knew the answer.

The princess started crying harder. 'My father is … My father was … You see I do not even know if he is still alive! Our neighbour

King Saleh attacked our kingdom without reason today. At best my father is now his prisoner.'

'Princess Giauhara, please do not cry. I am sure Saleh has no intention of killing your father.'

'But he has gone mad! My father always said he and his family were strange. He says they have spent too much time on land.'

It was becoming clear to Beder that Samandal said a lot of things, all of them negative.

'I promise you King Saleh has not gone mad,' he said. 'And he did not go to your kingdom in order to attack it.'

The princess had stopped crying. Now she was frowning at him. 'How do you know that?'

'I am King Beder. King Saleh is my uncle. He went to your kingdom in peace to ask your father to let me marry you.'

Giauhara backed away in alarm. 'You wish to *marry* me? Is that why you followed me here?'

'No!' said Beder, quickly. 'I mean, forgive me, you are lovely indeed, but … What are you doing?'

Giauhara had ripped off her shell necklace and now whispered something into it. As Beder watched, the wind picked up and the shell glowed green.

He felt a strange tingling all over his body. He held his hands up and watched as his fingers fused together. Then his arms and legs seemed to shorten as if they were being sucked into his torso. His eyesight doubled, but he could barely focus as Giauhara – who was suddenly a giant – picked him up with both hands and threw him into the air.

The wind caught Beder and swept him up. It took him to the mainland, although he did not know exactly where. He was on a beach that was covered in seagulls and other, long-legged birds with black and white feathers that stalked the sand for food. None of these birds were frightened of Beder because, as he was beginning to realise, he was no longer a man. Instead of a mouth he had a blue beak with blushes of orange and pink on either side. Instead of feet he had bright red webs.

And instead of arms he had white wings with dark brown tips.

The first thing he did, while the other birds watched, was try to fly. He needed to find Giauhara and get her to change him back into a man. But however much he flapped his new wings, the best he could do was a running jump and a brief glide – straight into the path of a local peasant.

'Help me!' said Beder, but all that came out was a squawk.

'What a beautiful bird you are!' said the peasant. 'Much too

peasant
A small-scale farmer of low status, with little education or money.

beautiful to eat …'

'Eat?' squawked Beder in alarm. He tried to fly away again, but the man caught him with a net, startling all the other birds into the sky.

Then he put Beder in a small wooden cage.

'I have caught and sold many birds, but I have never even seen one like you before,' the peasant said through the bars. 'I bet no one at the market has either.'

And if the looks Beder got as they walked into the city were anything to go by, the peasant was right. He attracted *lots* of attention.

'How much for the bird?' someone asked as soon as they arrived at the marketplace.

'How much will you give me?' asked the peasant, who did not know what price to put on such an unusual item.

'I will give you a silver coin.'

Another person called out, 'I will give you a gold one!' This was an incredible offer.

'Two!' said a third person.

And the price kept rising.

Each bidder snatched the birdcage from the last so that Beder was passed around the growing crowd in jerks and jolts. Voices rose and no one noticed a palanquin being carried towards them, or when it stopped so that the king of the area could see what had created such a frenzy in his market. He was just as impressed with the bird as everyone else.

'Four gold and one silver!' was the current bid, then–

'TEN GOLD COINS.'

The bidders finally looked

---

palanquin
A seat or box used as transport, carried by poles on the shoulders of several people.

towards the palanquin. As one they fell to their knees and pressed their foreheads to the ground. The birdcage dropped and rolled away.

Beder felt quite sick by now.

The unknown king sent a servant to pick up the birdcage and pay the peasant. Then he gave a signal for the men carrying him to move on. At his palace, he had Beder put in a magnificent cage in the dining room. The cage was big enough for ten birds, but of course Beder was not happy. It did not help that while Beder had only bird seed to eat, he watched the unknown king dine on bread and meat every mealtime.

And every mealtime, the unknown king felt that prickling

sensation on the back of his neck, the one you feel when you are being watched. Each time he looked up to find his new bird watching him. Finally, he approached the birdcage with food from his own plate, wandering if perhaps the bird was the meat-eating sort. He dropped some meat through the bars and Beder only looked at it. He was a king. He would not eat food off the floor.

'What do you want, then?' the unknown king asked him. 'Do you want to come out?'

He opened the birdcage and

reached in so that Beder could perch on his arm. From his arm, Beder jumped and soared clumsily to the empty place at the low dining table. There was a plate of saffron rice with a smattering of raisins and barberries, plus a whole leg of chicken that would have made Beder lick his lips if he still had them.

He tried to pick the chicken up in his webbed foot. Not only was the bone too thick for him to grasp, it was too hot. 'Ouch!' he squawked in pain. He hopped over to a cup of water so that he

might put his foot in it to cool it.
Afterwards he dried it on a napkin.

Watching all this from beside the
birdcage, the unknown king waved
at a servant. 'Fetch the
queen!' he hissed. 'I want
her to see this.'

The unknown queen arrived to see Beder flapping his wings to cool the food so that he might try eating it again.

'My dear,' said her husband, 'you know more about magic than I do. Am I right in thinking that this is no ordinary bird?'

'It is no bird at all! I believe it is a person.'

Beder stopped eating – or trying to eat. He squawked excitedly. 'Yes!'

'If that is true,' said the unknown king, unable to understand him; 'if you are indeed a person, lay one raisin and two barberries in front of you.' Quickly, Beder plucked the right berries from the rice with his beak and placed them on the table in front of him.

The unknown king was speechless, so his queen spoke for him. 'Using a raisin for yes and a barberry for no, tell me, are you King Beder of Persia?'

Beder gave another squawk and seized a raisin.

The unknown queen explained to her husband, 'I believe your new pet is none other than the son of the late King Hamid and the queen mother, Gulnare. Nephew of King Saleh of the sea and grandson of the former Queen Farasche. He has been missing for several days.'

'Can you change him back?'

'Of course.' The unknown queen took the cup that Beder had soothed his foot in. Over it she whispered, 'Quit this strange form and return to your natural shape

as a man.' Then she dipped her fingers in the water and sprinkled some over Beder. All at once his vision narrowed and his arms and legs seemed to stretch out from his chest. Afterwards, he held up his hands and wriggled his fingers.

'Now then,' said the unknown king, 'would you like to eat first, or explain how you came to be a bird?'

Chapter 6

The Story of King Beder and Queen Labe

In the end, King Beder did both, eating and explaining at the same time. The unknown king and queen were unknown no longer. They were King Akram and Queen Atifa, and Beder would never forget them for saving him. They were so shocked by his tale that they immediately offered to lend him their fastest ship home.

He gratefully accepted.

The ship sped forth for ten days, but on the eleventh day the wind changed. It became angry.

The ship was smashed against a rock, drowning most on board – but not Beder. While others survived by clinging to floating bits of wreckage, he was able to swim to shore, where he was grateful to see a large city in the distance. He hoped that someone there would help him continue his journey home to his mother.

As he began walking towards the city, however, Beder saw no

people on the road, only lots and lots of animals. There were horses, camels, donkeys, oxen, cows, bulls and more. They crowded round him and blocked his path, making all sorts of noises, from whinnying to bellowing. Some even bit his clothes to hold him back.

When he eventually made it to the city, he found the broad streets strangely empty. He came across some shops, which reassured him that the city must be inhabited after all. Then, finally, he came across a shopkeeper. It was an old man selling fruit.

'Good day,' Beder greeted him.

'Oh!' The fruit seller jumped in surprise, dropping several peaches to the floor. 'What are you doing here?'

'I–'

'You should not be here!' The fruit seller grabbed Beder and pulled him deeper into the shop, away from the open front. 'Did anyone see you?' he demanded.

'No,' said Beder. 'Nor did I see anyone – until you. Where are all the people?'

'Did you see the animals?'

'Yes! It was difficult getting past them.'

'Then you have seen most of the people, and you should not have tried to get past them. They were trying to save you. Now you may

suffer the same fate they did –
in fact I am surprised you made it
this far into the city without
her noticing.'

'Without whom noticing?'
asked Beder.

'The sorceress! Queen
Labe. She rules this
city as her mother did
before her. That means
she punishes those who
displease her by turning
them into animals or birds. It is
hard to believe, I know …'

Beder sighed. 'Not so hard.

---

sorceress
*A woman who claims or is believed to
have magic powers.*

Until recently I had been transformed into a bird. Tell me, how do people displease her?'

'No one knows,' the fruit seller said. 'It always starts well. Someone will catch her interest. She will invite them to spend time with her in the palace and treat them with utmost kindness. But by the end of forty days, they will be transformed. What about you? How did you come to be a bird?'

Beder told his story, after which the fruit seller said that he could stay with him.

'My name is Abdallah, and you are safer here than anywhere else in the City of Enchantments,' he promised. 'The queen knows me and has never taken enough of an interest for me to be in any danger. With luck, she will not notice you either. At least not before we can figure out a way for you to continue your journey home.'

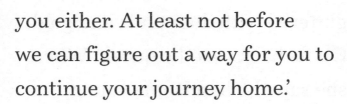

Abdallah was a respected man. When he told his neighbours that Beder was the son of his brother, they believed him. It was some time until Labe learnt of Beder's presence in her city, and it was by accident.

When he had been there for a month, Beder was sitting at the shop door when a troupe of guards dressed in purple appeared on horseback. In the middle of them was a magnificent horse that glittered with diamonds and gold. On its back was the queen. When she saw the handsome young Beder, she commanded her men to stop.

'Abdallah,' she called, until the

old man appeared. 'Who is this fine young man?'

'He is my nephew, Your Majesty. Although I look upon him more as a son.'

'You should have told me he was here,' said the queen. 'I would have welcomed him properly at the palace.'

Abdallah bowed apologetically. 'We are most grateful for Your Majesty's kindness, but there is no need. Young Beder considers himself lucky just to be in your fine city. There is no welcome necessary.'

Abdallah shot a fearful look at Beder. He could not refuse the queen, and everyone knew it, especially her.

'It is alright, uncle,' said Beder, who did not want to get the fruit seller into any trouble. 'It would be my pleasure to go with the queen.'

Riding behind one of the guards, Beder went with Labe to her palace. Along the way he noticed how the people they passed tried to hide from view, ducking inside doorways and closing window shutters. Those who did not hide

looked at the queen with hatred and Beder with pity.

'Poor stranger,' he heard them say more than once. 'No one is safe from her wickedness.'

But when they reached the palace, and the queen herself showed him inside, Beder was treated with great kindness.

'My home is your home,' she told him. 'Please, make yourself comfortable.'

This was not so difficult for Beder, who had grown up in a palace even finer than this one. To keep his identity secret, however, he remembered to compliment the size of the rooms, the fineness of the furniture and the beauty of the gardens. When they dined that evening on golden plates, he ate as if he had never eaten such delicious food before. The queen then served him even more food from her own plate.

Can this truly be the wicked sorceress I have heard so much about? Beder thought to himself. *I have never been so well treated!*

This treatment continued for over a month. Had Beder not been a king, with people to lead and work to do, he would have been content to stay longer. But he was a king, so when Labe asked at the end of forty days if he would stay with her, he had to refuse.

'I cannot thank Your Majesty enough for her kind attention,' he said, 'but I only came to visit my uncle and I have now been here longer than planned. I must return home.'

The queen was clearly very disappointed. Several expressions seemed to chase each other across her face. For a moment, Beder thought that one of them was anger.

But finally, she smiled.

'Very well, Beder, I understand. Tomorrow we will say goodbye. But you must stay for lunch – I have a surprise for you.'

That night, Beder lay awake in his bed. He was thinking, as he often did, about Princess Giauhara; only lately his thoughts held less anger and more understanding for her actions. He wondered if he would ever see her again, and what he would say if he did.

Suddenly, Beder heard a sound at his bedroom door. As he turned his head, he saw the door open and Labe tiptoe in. Then he closed his eyes and pretended to be asleep. The queen crept up to his bed. He felt two sharp tugs as she yanked two hairs from his head.

Afterwards Beder heard the door close and opened his eyes.

All at once, Beder remembered Abdallah's words and the people's hate-filled looks. What was the queen up to?

To find out, Beder left his bed and crept after her. He followed her to the palace kitchen and watched from the doorway. Labe poured water into a bowl and added flour to make a paste, and thereafter a cake. She added the two hairs from Beder's head to the cake mix. All the while, she muttered words he could not hear.

Hidden in the doorway, Beder swallowed nervously. The queen was clearly working her dark magic. If he was not careful, he would be transformed into an animal after all.

While the cake was baking, Beder ran to the queen's room and looked for her hairbrush. He plucked two hairs from it and returned to the kitchen in time to see the queen setting her cake aside to cool. Beder hid until she was gone, then he went inside. There was enough cake batter left in the mixing bowl to fill the baking tin again.

Quickly, because the night sky was already beginning to give way to day, Beder threw the first cake into the fire. Then he made a second, identical cake. The only difference was that Beder added the queen's hairs to the mixture and not his own. Then he set the

cake to cool and returned to his room. The next afternoon, he ate one last meal with Labe.

'I hope you do not mind,' she said. 'I am no cook, but I wanted to make you something with my own two hands to say thank you for your company these past weeks. Surprise!' And Labe presented Beder with the cake.

'But it is I who should be thanking *you*, Your Majesty,' he protested.

The queen pushed the cake towards him. 'You can thank me by eating some of this.'

Beder pushed the cake back. 'Only if you will eat some with me.'

'Very well,' she agreed, and she cut two slices. 'After you,' she said, signalling for Beder to eat first.

'No, no,' he said, 'after you.'

The queen began to look impatient. 'Perhaps we should eat at the same time?' she suggested.

'An excellent idea, Your Majesty!' So they each took a bite of cake and chewed. 'Delicious!' said Beder. But the queen had barely swallowed her mouthful before she leapt to her feet angrily.

'Ungrateful wretch!' she hissed,

dipping her hand in her cup and splashing water in Beder's face. 'Quit this form of a man and become a dog instead! Perhaps then you will show me some loyalty.'

There was an awkward silence in which nothing happened besides Beder drying his face and the queen turning red. When she realised that her magic had failed, she tried to hide what had happened.

'Forgive me,' she said. 'If I am honest, I am more upset about you leaving than I let on before.'

'I understand,' said Beder. 'Please, let me pour you some more water.'

But as Beder reached for the water jug, he did not pour from it. Instead, he dipped his hand inside and splashed it in the queen's face. 'Wicked sorceress!' he cried. 'Quit this form of a woman and become a – a …' Beder's mind raced. Should he say a dog too? A dog could be dangerous. His eyes searched the room and fell upon a tapestry of the queen's horse on the wall. 'A horse!' he finished.

Just like that, there was a beautiful horse and not a queen before him. Only then, as Labe kicked and shrieked in her new body, did Beder remember that a horse could be dangerous too. She charged at him with her blunt teeth bared, trampling furniture and churning up rugs, but he dodged and dashed out of the way. The sound of her hooves brought servants running to see what was happening.

'Bring me a rope,' Beder commanded.

A rope was swiftly brought and Labe the horse was secured. While she continued raging in the palace stables, Beder finally returned to Abdallah's shop. The old man hugged him.

'I thought I would never see you again!' he cried. 'How did you escape? What of Queen Labe?'

'Queen Labe cannot harm you anymore,' said Beder.

When he told Abdallah what had happened, the fruit seller wept tears of joy.

'But what about the people she has already harmed?' he wondered.

'How do we return them to their human bodies?'

'I have an idea,' said Beder. 'I will write to Queen Atifa, who changed me back from a bird. I am sure she will help. But first I must return home. I have been gone from my kingdom for too long.

'How will you travel?'

Beder grinned. 'By horse!'

Chapter 7

The Story of King Beder and Princess Giauhara Continued

When King Beder returned to the palace stables to saddle Queen Labe the horse, he expected a fight, and he got one. She reared up and kicked out. She almost bit him.

'Stop it,' Beder said, snatching his hand away just in time. 'This is for your own good. Your people hate you. If I leave you here, they may kill you. At least with me, as my horse, you will live.'

The horse stilled. She whinnied in a way that sounded like a question.

'Because I do not think you are all bad,' said Beder. 'I do not believe that all your kindness can be fake. Come with me, and I promise I will have you transformed back into a human along with all the poor people you punished. Deal?'

The horse tossed her head and pawed the ground.

'I will take that as a yes.'

Beder left the City of
Enchantments on horseback.
Within three days, he reached
another city where he stopped to
buy food and refill his water.
He left Labe the horse tied up
outside a shop. He returned to
find her surrounded by people.
Some were admiring her glossy
coat. Others were saying that she
had the perfect legs for racing.
One man had tried to check her
teeth and was now bleeding from
a bite on his arm.

'Excuse me,' said Beder, pushing
through. 'That is my horse.'

'How much for her?' said the man with the bleeding arm.

'Ignore him,' said an old woman he had not noticed before. '*I* will buy this horse.'

The man with the bleeding arm backed down immediately.

'The horse is not for sale,' Beder told her.

'I will give you ten gold coins,' said the old woman, who did not look rich enough to have even five gold coins to her name.

'I would like to help you,' said Beder, 'but I cannot.'

'Twenty gold coins.'

'No.'

'Fifty.'

'The horse is not for sale.'

'Name your price!'

Simply to be rid of her, Beder

named a price he thought she could not possibly afford.

'Fine,' he said: 'a thousand gold coins.'

'Deal!' said the old woman, and she put a heavy purse in his hand. 'Here is a hundred now. My house is nearby where I can get you the rest.'

Beder looked from the woman to the purse and back again. Her clothes were clean but not the latest fashion. Her hair was brushed but not styled. There was something familiar about her eyes that he could not place, but whatever it was, could she really have a thousand gold coins to spend on a horse?

'I was not being serious,' he said just in case. 'Please, let me pass. The horse is not for sale.'

'A deal is a deal!' said the woman. 'To break it means death around here. Does it not?' The people around her nodded quickly, almost fearfully.

So Beder followed the woman to her house to fetch the rest of the money, hoping that he could convince her not to buy the horse along the way.

'She is very bad tempered,' he said. 'And much older than you think.' Labe the horse glared at him for saying this.

'Please,' Beder begged. They had reached the old woman's house, which looked as plain and simple as she did. 'I really cannot sell you this horse – nor is it really a horse at all!'

'Oh, I know,' said the old woman. 'She is my daughter.'

The moment they stepped inside the stable, the old woman transformed into someone who looked just like Labe had looked, only older and more frightening. Labe the horse reared up. King Beder tried to run, but he was trapped. The woman dipped her hand into a horse trough and threw the water in his face.

'Young fool! Quit this form of a man and become something wiser!'

Beder felt the familiar sensation of his arms and legs shrinking and his eyesight doubling. He looked to see if he had wings again and his head turned almost full circle. Yes, he was a bird again. In fact, he was an owl.

The woman stuffed him into a tiny cage and turned to her daughter, the horse. 'And you!' she said. 'I left you in charge of the City of Enchantments and you fall victim to your own magic. Pathetic! Well, do not think I will change you back until you have learnt your lesson.'

Then she locked Labe the horse in a stall and left.

'Now I know why you are the way you are!' Beder the owl hooted.

'Now you know why I am the way I am!' Labe the horse neighed.

And neither one understood the other.

⊲▷⌦⌫⊲▷

Meanwhile, under the sea and on land, King Saleh and Gulnare had searched far and wide for Beder. Neither had found him, but the latter had found Princess Giauhara. She was brought to Gulnare in the palace by the sea.

'You will not remember me,' said Gulnare, 'but I knew you when you were a baby. I am Gulnare, Rose of the Sea.'

'And sister to King Saleh!' said

Giauhara angrily. 'The man who invaded my kingdom and killed my father!'

'You are wrong on both counts,' said Gulnare. 'My brother did not invade–'

'So King Beder told me!'

Gulnare gasped. 'You have seen Beder?'

Giauhara held her necklace and looked uncomfortable. 'Yes,' she admitted.

'Where is he? He has been missing for weeks!'

'If what you say is true and my father is still alive, then he has been a prisoner for weeks. If you give me my father, I will give you your son.'

Gulnare took the princess to Saleh, who met them in King Samandal's kingdom. The princess was relieved to find that her city had not changed, and shocked to see that the people had. They were actually *smiling*!

As much as she loved him, the princess knew that her father was far kinder to her than to his people. In the past she had tried to be twice as good to the people to make up for her father, but it never worked. Now it seemed that the people were happier under Saleh's rule.

'Take me to my father,' Giauhara demanded when the other king greeted her. She expected him to bargain for information about his nephew, but to her surprise he did as she asked. To her greater surprise, Samandal was not in the prison, but in his own room.

'Father!' she cried, throwing herself into his arms

'Giauhara!'

---

bargain
To bargain for something is to offer an exchange of money, goods, information or services. The goal is to make the terms of an agreement or trade better for yourself, often by giving less or getting more.

'Are you well, father?'

'I am. King Saleh has been kinder than I deserve.'

Giauhara blinked at these words. 'That does not sound like you! I thought you disliked King Saleh?'

Samandal laughed bitterly. 'Daughter, can you name anyone I do *not* dislike?'

The princess could not. 'But how can you call him kind when he holds you prisoner in your own kingdom?' she asked.

'I am no prisoner. True, there was a guard at my door to begin with, but now I am free to come and go as I please. I choose to stay in here.'

'Why?'

'How can I face the people now that I know how much they hate me? They abandoned me, daughter! And I do not blame them. I have been a terrible king.'

'But you can do better, father. I will help you.'

'First, we must return King Beder to his family, or there will be no peace between us. Is it true that you know where he is?'

Giauhara shook her head guiltily. 'No. But I can try to find out.'

Saleh and Gulnare were called into the room, where Giauhara revealed that she had turned Beder into a bird.

'But,' she said, before Gulnare could worry even more, 'the spell was broken some time again. I felt it happen through my necklace.'

Giauhara's necklace had been a gift from a sea witch. As the others watched, she whispered a summoning spell into it that would bring Beder to them. But it did not work.

Giauhara frowned. 'A stronger magic must be keeping him where he is,' she said. 'I will try a finding spell instead.'

She whispered into the shell again, and this time it glowed and floated up in front of her, tugging gently at her neck until she followed. Quickly, everyone else did too, including her father, Saleh and men and women from both their kingdoms.

The necklace led them far across the sea, lighting their way as day became night and night became day. Finally, they reached a shore. The land beyond it was covered in animals, but the city beyond that was strangely quiet. The first person they saw was an old man in a fruit shop.

'Excuse me,' said Gulnare. 'We are looking for a young man who might have come this way. His name is Beder.'

Abdallah the fruit seller lowered his voice and winked. 'Do you mean *King* Beder?'

'Yes!' said Gulnare, quickly translating for everyone who did not speak the language, including Giauhara.

Abdallah explained that Beder had left some days ago, towards the nearest city. Then he recognised the princess, whom Beder had once grudgingly described as beautiful.

'Your son promised that he would return and transform the people back to their human bodies, but perhaps the princess can do it now instead?'

The princess was horrified to learn that all the animals they had passed on their way there were really humans, and she could not believe that she had once worked such an evil spell herself. She instantly set about transforming the animals back to humans. Afterwards they kissed her hands and blessed her, until she forgot to fear them as her father had once said she should.

Land people do not seem so greedy and dangerous to me, she thought.

In the next city over, the shell necklace glowed brighter than ever. They asked after a young man on horseback and were directed towards the old woman's house.

'But be careful,' the people warned them. 'She is a sorceress.'

Sorceress or not, the woman was no match for an army – let alone two of them. As they broke through the doors, they saw the old woman disappear, leaving her daughter behind as she had so many times in the past. Indeed, she was the reason why Labe always tried so hard to make people love her, and reacted so badly when they wanted to leave.

'Beder?' cried Gulnare, the second she found the owl in the stable. 'Is that you?'

When the owl hooted in confirmation, Giauhara whispered into her necklace. 'Quit this strange form and return to your natural shape as a man.'

Human again, Beder hugged his mother. Then he seized Giauhara's hands in both of his.

'Please, help my friend here,' he said, pointing to Labe the horse.

'But is she not the sorceress who transformed everyone in the last city into animals?'

'She is,' said Beder, 'but everyone makes mistakes.'

At first, the princess thought these words were about her, highlighting *her* mistake in turning him into a bird. Then she realised that Beder was looking pointedly at his uncle and her father.

'Please,' he said again. 'I believe Labe has learnt her lesson.'

Giauhara did as she was asked.

Afterwards Labe returned to the city she had wronged to try to make up for it.

'If you can forgive me,' she told Beder, 'perhaps with time they can too. Maybe I can earn their love truly one day.'

Beder wished her good luck and returned to the underwater kingdoms with the sea people.

Working together to rescue Beder had healed some of the damage between his family and Giauhara's, but he was keen to do more. He started visiting Samandal and his daughter every week, even after he returned to the surface. At first, Samandal insisted on being there all the time, but eventually, he left Beder and Giauhara alone together.

'My father spends more time listening to the people's problems than he used to,' the princess told him. 'Both he and the kingdom seem happier for it.'

'They have come a long way,' Beder agreed. 'As have we.'

'Yes! From neighbours to enemies to friends.'

'But you know,' said Beder, 'I would like to be even more.'

'As would I,' said Giauhara. 'But you once said that you did not want to marry me.'

'And you once turned me into a bird.'

'That again?' Giauhara rolled her eyes playfully. 'I will forgive you if you forgive me.'

'How about you marry me if I marry you?'

'Deal!' said Giauhara, and they sealed it with a kiss. Bringing land and sea together once more.